Ian Whybrow Tim Warnes

Say Hello
to the
Dinosaurs

MACMILLAN CHILDREN'S BOOKS

Are you ready with your roars?
Let's say hello to the dinosaurs!

Stegosaurus has plates on his back.
He swishes his tail as he stamps down the track.

What a long way from your tail to your nose!
You're Diplodocus, I suppose!

Hello, Diplodocus!

Chomp, chomp, chomp!

Spinosaurus opens his jaws.
He waves his fan and his shiny claws.

Under the sea and close to the shore,
Swims a fishy Ichthyosaur.

Hello, Ichthyosaur!

Bubble, bubble!

Three pterodactyls glide in the sky.
Little ones hide when they fly by!

Hello, Pterodactyl!

Kaaark, kaaark, kaaark!

Triceratops is hard to beat,
With his three big horns and powerful feet!

Here's the fiercest of them all.
Listen to my mummy's call!

Hello, Tyrannosaurus!

ROOAAARRR!

Now we'll play a little game.
I'll ask a question and you say the name!

Who's the longest dinosaur
in this book?

Which dinosaur has a fan
on his back?

Who's got a spiky tail that goes
swish, swash, swish?

Who swims under the sea going **bubble, bubble?**

Who flies up high calling **kaaark, kaaark, kaaark?**

Who has very sharp teeth and a hungry roar?

Who looks like a rhino, but with three horns?

Did you enjoy that? Want some more?
Then say so like a dinosaur!

For Milo Benwell-Froggatt – I.W.

For the mighty Levisaurus,
and long-lost Dinosaur Jack – T.W.

First published 2009 by Macmillan Children's Books
This edition published 2019 by Macmillan Children's Books
an imprint of Pan Macmillan
20 New Wharf Road, London N1 9RR
Associated companies throughout the world
www.panmacmillan.com

Find out more about Ian Whybrow and Tim Warnes' books at
www.ianwhybrow.com and www.chapmanandwarnes.com

Pan Macmillan does not have any control over, or any responsibility for,
any author or third-party websites referred to in or on this book.

ISBN: 978-1-5098-8554-1

Text copyright © Ian Whybrow 2009
Illustrations copyright © Tim Warnes 2009
Moral rights asserted.

135798642

A CIP record for this book is available from the British Library.

Printed in Spain

Dinosaurs